Reader's

Praise for *The Note*

Enjoy at your own risk!

The story was gripping, the emotional turmoil facing Eddie was palpable throughout. You felt the tense nervousness gripping him over the few short hours the story covers. The dialogue is believable, clear, without affectations and not contrived.

A new master's in Thriller Town and he's here to stay. A pulse-quickening, brain-teasing adventure. Thriller writing doesn't get any better than this.

Eddie quickly becomes a friend, someone who you listen to and understand - someone to trust.

The Note and *The Lift* do not feel like short stories. They are carefully crafted glimpses into the unique world of Eddie Collins.

This is a fast paced, hard to put down story. It kept me up late into the night as I needed to see the outcome.

Sarcasm and black humour, action aplenty, this is a winner.

Power-packed, explosive introduction to Eddie Collins.

Andrew Barrett writes with a word paint brush and really takes you into the story he's painting! This one is dark, claustrophobic, exciting, startling, with flashes of humour and a surprise ending which I didn't see coming.

What a gripping read I loved it.

I felt I was actually there with Eddie, although he didn't listen to me when I told him to RUN.

Great short story full of action and suspense. Will definitely read the full stories of CSI Collins

Every time you think you have something figured out you are so wrong. If this were a movie you would be at the edge of your seat.

I loved this Eddie story and I want his dictionary! Eddie says and thinks what we would like to say and do.

Eddie's frustration with Officer 'Dibble' is a joy, I love his sarcasm. A brilliant story with an extra twist at the end that I did not anticipate.

If you like a little shiver, and the hairs standing up on the back of your neck, you can't go wrong here!

Throughout the story the suspense is ratcheted up, until it is almost palpable, and only relieved by Eddie's irreverence and (nervous) wisecracks. I really like the Eddie character, he is human and believable and has a healthy dose of mistrust for authority,

I love Eddie Collins. He is one of my favourite characters and I do struggle with the idea that he's not real.

There is a lot of dark humour in this which had me laughing aloud.

If you're looking for a short story that grips you from the first page....look no more, you've found it.

The Note is jam packed with drama, hard hitting and often brutal scenes, twists and turns abound make this a highly charged story.

THE NOTE

A CSI Eddie Collins short story

by

ANDREW BARRETT

— The Scene —

Do you ever have that feeling of being watched, and when you turn around, no one's there? Spooky, isn't it? It happened to me tonight, and I wish I'd taken more notice; I wish I'd looked harder.

I was working a half-night shift. That means I start work at 6pm and go home around 2am. I say 'around' because often I'll be late off – this is the police, after all. Working as a CSI in Leeds means there's plenty to keep me occupied on this shift.

My Control Room sent me to a scene in some pub car park in the shittiest end of Leeds that was so dilapidated it made Beirut look like Chelsea. And despite the rain, I would be the entertainment to a group of toothless drunken men for two and a half hours.

They kept going inside for a fresh beer and coming back out to watch me again, maybe hoping I'd done something wonderful like pull a murderer out of a top hat, or found their missing teeth. Christ, didn't these people have lives? I suppose if they did, they'd be living them, right? Arseholes.

Anyway, the scene consisted of a dead guy who was curled into a foetal position about a yard from the pub's gable-end wall, which was good really because it offered a bit of protection from the rain. Near to him was a length of scaffolding pole, and draining from the flap in his scalp was a pool of blood the size of a welcome mat.

The paramedics had pronounced life extinct, and were just wrapping up; their green uniforms dark and shiny because of the rain. You could see in their eyes that they just wanted to be away now they'd done their bit. And on a night like this who could blame them?

The only copper there seemed surprised to see me. He explained that when this incident happened none of the pissheads were in the car park. So details were sketchy at best, but it seemed that this guy had walked from the pub and some lowlife had jumped him. Couldn't see yet if he still had his wallet on him, so I couldn't rule robbery out.

And actually it wouldn't surprise me if one of those giggling pissheads over there was the killer, just watching me, proud of his handiwork, maybe wondering if I was smart enough to pull *him* out of the hat! The copper had a brief word with the PCSO on the tape and then waltzed off inside the pub, pulling out his pocket notebook as he went.

Judging by CIDs lack of presence, they obviously weren't keen to come out and play on account of the rainwater would dissolve them, I guess. They were probably playing cards back in the nick where it was warm and dry: loser gets to brave the rain and take statements from the drunken soup-drinkers.

So I had a scene rapidly being washed away, a gawping, shouting mob standing behind a piece of thin blue and white tape less than ten yards away. I also had a young PCSO trying to keep them on the far side of it without getting drunk on their breath or being vomited on. I *did* say it was the shittiest part of Leeds.

I too was anxious to be away, but I was determined to do a thorough job. I wanted to make sure

The Note

I'd done everything I could do to catch the bastard and help the victim's family get justice.

That must sound like public relations bullshit to you, but you should know I don't do PR – we have a department for that. I just do the best I can, that's all the PR I give. I'm also paid to do the best job I can, and doing anything less would be theft, really. And I'm not a thief.

And I expect it sounds like a back-covering exercise too, but it really isn't. This job, shit though it is sometimes, is there to help victims of crime – whether those victims are themselves innocent or not. Either way, this guy might have kids, and they'd have to grow up knowing their dad was murdered and the killer was still free, that the police had failed them.

So I was prepared to get wet and listen to drunken renditions of *Who Are You?* I was prepared to do the job right. It's a process. And you could either follow it and capture everything that was there to capture, or you could just flit around looking for the obvious and miss the more subtle clues entirely. That's the difference between a good examiner doing a good job and a shit examiner pretending to do a good job.

Things like the scaffolding pole leap out at you; they're obvious and yes, they could lead to an offender very quickly. But overlook something like offender's blood on the victim, offender's hair on the victim, offender's footwear marks in the victim's blood, and you suddenly become reliant upon that scaffolding pole giving you the answer.

On a job like this one, the investigators rely on forensic evidence to get them ahead in the game. There's only forensic evidence and circumstantial evidence at play here, seeing as there are no witnesses. And if I miss the forensic evidence, there's no suspect. Game over.

The PCSO at the cordon looked around at me as I set up my camera, and shouted the words everyone who's trying to concentrate loves to hear, "How long are you going to be?"

This angered me almost as much as the rainwater trickling down the back of my neck. "Piece of string," I said.

And that insignificant exchange seemed to be the trigger for a drunken arsehole to get his two-penn'orth in and rise in the ranks of arseholedom. "Gill Grissom would've caught the bastard by now." His drinking companions thought this was hysterical. I didn't. But I ignored them and got on with taking the initial scene shots with a few yellow markers laid out next to those pertinent bits of evidence. I wanted to get to the body as quickly as I could, but you can't ignore the preliminary things.

And one of those preliminary things included getting a tent up over the deceased as quickly as possible. If you've ever put up a marquee in your back garden, you'll know it's almost impossible to do by yourself, so I was hoping that CID had finished playing cards by now, or some backup for the PCSO and the copper might show up before this place succumbed to a drunken uprising or my corpse floated off down the street.

Once I'd taken the initial photos, I couldn't resist a quick peep at the body, just in case there *was* that stray hair lying in a vulnerable place that even a small breeze could carry off. I squatted at the dead man's side and glided the torchlight over him.

He was only a few feet from the pub wall, and about as far from a broken fence too. Beyond the fence and growing through it were nettles and bracken that had trapped fast-food wrappers, empty beer cans, and masses of cigarette ends. I could have used a cigarette myself, but I resisted the urge, keen to get on with the job.

The slugs appeared from nowhere, dozens of them, unable to resist *their* urge to drink their fill of the dead man's blood – I'd known those little bastards ruin blood spatter patterns before now. And even though there was no danger of that here – it was just a lake, no patterns – I couldn't help but shudder at the sight of them, so I went back to studying the dead man.

There was nothing remarkable about him: he was mid-thirties, white, short dark hair (now very red towards the back), wearing old jeans, a green t-shirt, and a fleece. His eyes were open, and death had gifted that familiar opacity like he had a bad case of cataracts, and the rain had clumped his eye lashes together. The whole mess of his face gave me a strange sensation.

I recognised him from somewhere.

Making out his facial features was a pain because of all the blood from a second wound across his cheek, but I recognised the crucifix earring and the mobster moustache. When I stood up, I also recognised the red Nike trainers he'd been wearing when I saw him last.

And that's when things turned sour.

A plain car pulled up outside the pub and the longcoats got out. CID. These are the coppers who chase clichés. They're the ones who see what a detective looks like on the telly and try to imitate them, creating a fake image from a fake image. A counterfeit counterfeit, a self-perpetuating caricature. They're plastic, and I could tell by the way they swaggered over to me that they were thinking of their image for the crowd.

Like Morse and Lewis they ducked under the tape and nodded as they approached; the temperature dropped by ten degrees just because they were so fucking cool. I gritted my teeth, and stopped work again. It was difficult to tell who they were to begin with, with their collars pulled up against the drizzle, but my heart sank as I saw him.

"DS Trafford," he said to the PCSO, a little too loudly, and then looked at his audience, hoping to soak up some wows or oohs. Only mockery was forthcoming. He looked like a bad drawing of Officer Dibble. I didn't like him. Never had. For six months or more he'd worked the same shift pattern as I did, and each time he came to a job of mine I would sigh because he wasn't off sick or hadn't been demoted to tuck shop attendant.

I didn't recognise his buddy, but judging by the matching longcoat he was obviously emulating Dibble in the hope of scoring Brownie points. Creep. Dibble didn't introduce me to him, but he was short, face like a bashed crab.

I don't like strangers showing up at my scenes. I said to Dibble, "You lost at snap, then?"

"I beg your pardon."

"Never mind."

"We're locking it down. Tent it and you can go."

"What?" I admit that I was a bit flabbergasted by this, but refused to let someone I didn't like mess me around at a scene that warranted a decent job. "My scene. I'm working it." The crowd was getting drunker, louder, just a confusion of noise that chipped away at the edges. "You don't want a scene on overnight with that lot hanging around."

Dibble wasn't accustomed to being challenged; you could tell that by his face, how it screwed up as though his tongue had turned into a lemon. I think he was expecting me to say 'Oh gee, thanks', and wheel-spin my way back to the nick.

"We're locking it down till daylight."

I had no intention of locking it down. There were things that needed doing tonight, and if he wanted to leave the stiff there until daylight and give the slugs a real feast, then fine, he could have it. But I was going to tent it and process the rest of the scene.

And I even knew who the dead guy was!

It's every DS's dream to have an identity to work with right from the off, but there was more chance of him finding a personality in a box of Kellogg's Cornflakes than he had of me giving him that piece of good news. Let the prick try to get it out of this rabble, and see how far he gets.

His idea was to come here, look cool as he fired off a few orders, take a couple of statements and then prepare a briefing pack for the poor bastards who had to work it the next day. Like I said, you only need to lose evidence once and you've got a murderer skipping down the beach singing *Oh What a Beautiful Morning*. "Just a minute," I stepped even closer, not in a confrontational kind of way, just trying to keep my voice down a bit, "You give me a hand to tent it, and then you can go and take your statements and avoid whatever else needs doing. Leave the rest to me."

"Goodbye." Dibble and Bashed-Crab turned and walked towards the PCSO.

I stood there like a prick, like a kid who'd just had his sandwiches taken off him by a bully. I felt more than a little embarrassed, but that feeling was a pebble compared to the mountain of anger that crashed over me. "Oi, Dibble!"

They both stopped in unison, and turned to face me. It was almost graceful. The crowd quietened, the way people do when they sense an atmosphere, something untoward developing.

"Ayup, Quincy's in a mood." The newly crowned King of Arseholedom began laughing at his own joke, and soon the rest were laughing along with him, like it was a toothless grin parade at a hick festival.

"Quincy," I shouted, "is a fucking pathologist, you prick."

The crowd jeered, and then Dibble was in my face, close enough so I could see the flecks of rain landing on his perfectly trimmed eyebrows. "What did you say?"

"Quincy. He's a pathologist."

"What is your name?"

I looked at him, and confusion somehow dissipated my anger. This wasn't a friendly 'what do they call you?' question; this was an 'I need your name for the complaint I'm about to file' question. "My name?"

"I have dismissed you from the scene, and you have seen fit to stir the crowd with a derisive comment."

"How often have we worked scenes together, and you don't know my name?" I looked at Bashed-Crab, "Is he serious?"

Dibble answered for him. "Last time of asking. What is your name?"

I cleared my throat, he *was* serious. "Bill," I said. "Bill Gristle."

He actually took out a notebook and a pencil and wrote it down. "Thank you, Bill," he said, nodding towards the body. "You can tent it and go."

The disbelief in Bashed-Crab's eyes was a delight. He nudged Dibble, and then whispered something. I stood there with my arms folded and a grin on my face as realisation grew on his. Dibble looked pissed off and took a small step up to me. "Funny man, eh? I will be taking this further." He gritted his teeth and spoke through them, "Stop fucking about and do as I say or things will get messy for you."

Oops. Threats and me never really got on too well, and I took a small step forward too, just enough to bring my boot gently down on his patent leather toe and prevent him from reversing. I brought my face down to his level, curled his beautiful silk tie into my fist, and growled, "You wanna put in a complaint because I refuse to compromise evidence? Fine, go ahead, I'll argue all day long with your Inspector. But threaten me again and I'll punch your slimy brown tongue so far down your throat you'll be able to taste your own fear. Got it?"

"Get your fucking—"

"And I don't care for rank either, so try pulling that shit on me and see how far it gets you. Now get out of my scene." The crowd was almost silent, even the PCSO was looking, and I could see Bashed-Crab cringe as he studied the raindrops on his shiny shoes.

Dibble attempted and failed to straighten his tie, and even from here I could feel the heat burning on his flushed cheeks. "You haven't heard the last of this."

See what I mean about Mr Cliché?

I smiled, and mouthed 'fuck off'. He did, and the crowd parted as the red-faced man with the crumpled tie barged his way through.

Ten minutes later a police van with two coppers on board pulled up, and I enlisted their help in erecting the scene tent and positioning it over the body. Now I was happy.

Bashed-Crab and Dibble had either gone or they were still in the pub regaining their composure by taking statements and ordering drunks around. The crowd had thinned considerably, and the PCSO hadn't muttered a word to me. Bliss. Now I could get on with the job.

The Note

— The Note —

I got back to the office and dumped a shitload of exhibits – including his wallet – on my desk. My back ached and I was wet through. But I could relax in the knowledge that I had done my job, and I had helped the investigators with things that might otherwise have been lost when the day shift came on. I made sure that little snippet went into the report – now *that's* watching your back!

His name was John Tyler. And I recalled him quite clearly because he was a man I had photographed only two days before he was beaten to death. We take domestic violence seriously and often photograph injuries to victims, male and female. This man was a shy fellow, embarrassed by his predicament, and by the bruises all over his body. I had felt bad for him, as I do with all victims of domestic abuse.

I also wondered, as you do, if this guy had asked for it in the first place, or if he had retaliated afterwards. But his knuckles were bruise-free and so I concluded that he hadn't, deciding that he was too meek to do either. I'd applauded him for being brave enough to ask for help.

But what really book-marked him in my mind were the bite marks. He'd had, as I recall, a prominent one spanning the bridge of his nose, fresh too, the bruising not yet fully developed. I remember thinking what a bastard that will be to photograph correctly, and I also remember thinking how it must have made his eyes water.

He had several more: one on his right shoulder and another on his right wrist. Both of those were bad enough to have drawn blood. I imagined the kind of frenzied attack he must have suffered in order to get bitten and beaten like that; but if you want the truth, I didn't have to imagine too hard. It's happened to me, thanks to an old girlfriend. I've been bitten and punched; almost lost an eye thanks to her nails. She was vile.

And so I had a real empathy for Mr Tyler, and felt more than a little sadness for him now that I knew how his life ended. All we had to do now was work out who had ended it, and why.

* * *

Ever had a death threat?

I've had several. Most of them are just plain silly, fired off by young men who've been caught doing something they shouldn't by the nice man with the fingerprint brush. They can't handle the embarrassment of being caught, or they're angry with themselves for making elementary errors in their execution of a naughty deed. You do the crime, you do the time, as the saying goes.

I file those threats in the bin, metaphorically speaking of course. In reality I hand them over to an equally nice police officer who sees to it that the author is reprimanded for his almost inevitable spelling and grammatical errors alongside the threat itself.

Either way, I don't dwell on them. How often have you said, 'I'm going to kill you!' in a fit of temper? If you're anything like me, you'll say that pretty much every day because there's always someone worthy of the imaginary pistol you have in your pocket

– always someone worthy of beating to a pulp – Dibble being a prime example. So these threats are just those kids pointing their finger pistol at me. Que sera; I let it go.

Then there are the not quite so silly ones. The ones that wipe the ever-present smile from my face. The one I received tonight was just such a threat. The letter I had in my sweaty little hand right now caused me to forget all about John Tyler, and stare at it. I swear my hair stood up a little just as a creeping tingling feeling radiated my body.

It was one o'clock in the morning, and the chances of me getting a bit of a flier looked good. I'd eaten my meal, brought my computer-work more or less up-to-date, and I began getting my Inbox down to a level where I could see over the top of it without needing a step ladder. Even after the clash with Dibble, I was relaxed, chilled out, and there was no one left in the office to piss me off – even my prick of a boss had done one, and so all was well with the world. Until I opened this letter.

I stared at it.

I reached for my coffee only to discover the cup was empty and cold. I hate that! And now I needed a cigarette. I stared at it some more. It said:

Your going to die tonight.

The spelling alone filed it away into the plain silly category, but what pulled it back and made me take notice was the paper it was scrawled on. It was torn, it was stabbed, ripped. If you could be pissed off with a sheet of A4 this is what it would look like. And I could imagine the author's fury because those stab marks were made, not by the pen nib, but by a knife.

I swallowed, looked up at the office door, then looked around the office. I have no idea why, unless part of me thought it was a shit practical joke and the author was watching me, giggling behind his hand.

I then did what I should have done after first opening it; I slid it carefully inside an evidence bag and sealed it. I wondered how long it had been sitting in my tray. There was no postal stamp on it, so it had been hand-delivered. The title simply said, 'Eddie Collins, CSI', in the same handwriting, and using the same pen. The envelope was a self-adhesive type, so he hadn't licked the flap or anything so useful. The envelope went into another bag, and I went for a smoke, looking around all the while.

I usually walk to my smoking spot with my eyes down so as to avoid any chance of someone stopping to talk to me. But this time, I was on full alert, looking everywhere, scrutinising the faces of the few people I passed along the way. It must have looked very suspicious.

I don't mind admitting that it played on my mind. After I finished the cigarette, I lit up another and noticed my hands tremble ever so slightly under the lights in the back car park. Behind me was utter blackness as the car park stretched on for hundreds of yards behind the nick. No lights up there, only here by the entrance. There were noises coming from inside the blackness, and I edged away from them, smoked a little faster.

The rain had slowed to a drizzle as though it were the backdrop to my feelings, mirroring them, running in parallel. I knew there'd be a deluge before long.

Your going to die tonight.

"Wish I knew when 'tonight' was, exactly," I said to no one as I walked back inside, feeling the dampness seeping through my clothes. Did they mean tonight, as in the day they'd delivered it - yesterday? In which case they'd already missed their deadline. Or did they mean tonight as in the day that was just over an hour old?

It didn't really matter, I concluded. If they didn't kill me within the next twenty-three hours, I was hardly likely to sue under the Trades Descriptions Act. Naturally, my mind then slid along to *how* they were going to despatch me. And in truth I wondered lots more things for the next forty-five minutes, mostly unpleasant things.

I found that the silence I usually adored had become somehow oppressive, claustrophobic. I could hear everything as though I had an amplifier strapped to my head. My boots shushing on the dirty office carpet, the creak of the store room door hinges, the echo in the little anteroom as I put the evidence bags away. It really didn't help my nerves that the lights were flickering. It was all coming together to make a bad horror movie. But I was nervous. I tried to laugh – refused to whistle though – but that only made me more nervous.

I swallowed nothing, sat back at my desk, and emailed my prick of a boss to let him know the letter and envelope needed to go for chemical treatment. And then it was time to go home.

I opened the office door straight into a copper's face! It was one of those moments where neither party wanted to appear scared but both jumped anyway. He shouted, "Wanker," and I shouted, "Fuck!" Just one of those immediate reaction things, nothing personal.

We smiled as though sharing some secret, and then passed each other by. I would've smirked on my way down the corridor, but my heart was still busy climbing back up my rib cage, and anyway, I had more serious things to ponder. However, I thought his choice of surprise expletive, 'wanker', was rather convoluted for such an immediate situation. 'Shit' is always a good one to fall back on: single syllable, rolls off the tongue. 'Wanker', strange choice. If you look up 'wanker' in the (Eddie) Collins dictionary you'd see: *n taboo slang, a worthless or stupid person, esp Audi-driver or boss.*

I turned off my radio, put it away in the locker on the hallway wall – one of hundreds more just like it, and collected my house key and my car key. The cool night air and thin drizzle refreshed my face as though someone had just slapped me. And still I wondered if I was being watched.

As I climbed into the Discovery, I admit to looking in the back seats before I turned the ignition. Silly, I know, but I was spooked; you'd have done the same. And as I let the car wend its own way home, my mind drifted a little, and then BANG! I had one of those moments that almost saw me drive off the fucking road and into a ditch.

I recognised that hand writing.

Only five words. But I was sure I'd seen it before somewhere. If I recognised it, then I must know the person who wrote it, right? It wasn't like one of those silly death threats where some kid I've never met before gets hold of my name and just tries to be cute; this guy *knew* me. And I knew him.

The Note

My mind went off at some peculiar tangent, studying the list of people I knew. It wasn't an overly long list, but I thought I'd shorten it further by erasing those who weren't pissed off at me. It didn't grow much shorter if the truth be told. I'm not one of life's cuddly sorts. Sorry. While my mind was playing with faces, I'd totally forgotten the obvious fact. If someone was serious about killing me, they couldn't really wish for a better place to do it than my house.

It's a single-storey cottage half way along a dead end road in the middle of nowhere. And I live alone. It's my overt way of saying that I prefer my own company. The only visitors I get are the ones I invite: usually pizza delivery.

Before I knew it, I had turned off the main drag and followed the lane until the turning for my dead end road appeared on my left. No time for a reccy now; I'd blown it by simply driving straight to my house. I sighed and mentally slapped my face for being so stupid.

No wonder they declined my Mensa application.

The good news was that the headlights didn't pick out any vehicle, and there was nobody about – that I could see. The bad news was that the headlights didn't pick out any vehicle and there was nobody about – that I could see. My mouth was as dry as Ghandi's flip-flop, and my palms were squeaking on the steering wheel.

It had worked; if the note was a tactic designed to scare me a little, it had worked, and the author had scored his little victory and could sleep soundly knowing he'd won. Yet, he couldn't. Because he wouldn't *know* he'd won. Unless he was watching me. That strange tingling feeling in the back of my neck returned.

I drove to the end of the road, did an eight-point turn and drove slowly back along to the cottage. Still nothing. I swallowed but my throat was as dry as my mouth. I could kill for a beer right now. Two would be better. I lit a cigarette instead.

Now what?

It all boiled down to how seriously I took this threat. If I genuinely thought a madman had sent the letter with every intention of carrying it out, I would be curled up in a Holiday Inn by now, locked in the bathroom with a coffee and one of those little brown biscuits. So, had I subconsciously discounted the threat? Or had I rated it as highly unlikely to occur? Great, my subconscious mind was making decisions that *I* had to live with!

I left the headlights on and climbed out of the Discovery. There was a streetlamp at the end of the road, but seriously, even with his head up his arse, my boss could see better. So, casting a pair of long black shadows before me, I headed through the stillness to the front door, and cursed not having the intelligence to bring home my Maglite. As predicted, the rain had indeed grown a little heavier, I could hear it pattering on the sleeves of my jacket, and could hear the long grass dancing in the breeze.

I was getting really quite jittery, and wondered if I should get the hell inside quickly, or go and look around the house first to see if I could see any point of entry.

From somewhere nearby an owl laughed at me.

Deciding whether to check things out was one of those questions to which there isn't really a right or wrong answer – just varying degrees of error; I still had Holiday Inn in mind.

If I checked around and found something wrong, a forced or broken window, I'd hightail it out of here – much better than being inside when the would-be killer decided to demonstrate how serious he was about fulfilling his threat.

It was while I peeked around the far wall where all the nettles and cow parsley grow rampant, that it occurred to me. I mean I couldn't see shit anyway, so coming around here was a bad idea after all. Anyway, it occurred to me: why send a death threat at all?

If you're going to kill someone, you don't want them to be prepared! You want them to be oblivious to it; you want it to be a smooth and satisfying experience, surely! If you prepare someone, it's likely to go tits up. Unless it's me you're threatening, of course – in which case I seemed to be doing everything I could to make it go smoothly for you. Hate to disappoint. Goes to show how little I know or appreciate about the complexities of other people's minds.

To me life is pretty straight-forward. Live it. Get angry. Live it.

That's how you live life to the full, by experiencing it, and by experiencing the delight that anger gives to you. Anger is therapeutic and pure; it's the medicine that keeps me sane. I suspect it also gives me high blood pressure, but you can't have it all.

Smoke curled up my face and stung my eyes, and the glowing end hissed with each droplet of rainwater. I tossed the cigarette aside and listened. All that came back was the laughing owl and the gentle swishing of weeds singing in a breeze. There was only darkness around here.

But on the other hand, to send out a death threat could destabilise the victim into making your job as a killer a whole lot easier. And it's the trap I just fell arse over tit into.

That was about the point when anger took over the situation. I was tired after a long shift, and all I'd thought about for the last couple of hours was how some arsehole had taken root in my mind (making me forget, incidentally, to get milk on the way home!), some arsehole who didn't know the difference between *your* and *you're*. Prick!

Time to stop pussyfooting around. I marched around the front of the house, pulling my house key out of my pocket, and used the light from the Discovery to help me stuff it in the lock. Sick of feeling nervous – okay, sick of feeling *afraid*, I opened the door quickly, letting it thud into the wall with a hefty bang.

Blackness greeted me. Familiar smells of stale coffee and very stale cigarette smoke. Home. I prodded the light switch but nothing happened. Still blackness.

Fuck.

Don't get me wrong, I was still angry because this was turning out to be a major inconvenience. It was also scaring the living shit out of me. But the anger moved aside now and fear crept in, nudging its way to the front of the queue with alarming silkiness. Of course, the fuse had blown, that was all. Or there was a power cut; nothing to get alarmed about.

The Note

Now I don't really get along too well with the notion of coincidence, so that, added to the death threat made a night at Holiday Inn so very appealing. Of course I still wasn't sure there was anything to run away from yet, but I was aware that by the time I found out there *was* something to run away from, it would be too late to do anything about it.

Call me a scaredy cat, I don't care what you think; I wanted to get the hell out of there as fast as I could. I reached in to grab the door handle, to close the door and lock it, when I heard it.

— The Terror —

"Eddie."

I held my breath and stood perfectly still. I stared into the blackness beyond the door, aware of the Discovery only ten yards behind me lighting me up like that proverbial bad guy in the horror movie, come to dispatch you with his axe. Except this was a slight role reversal, I admit.

I saw the tip of a cigarette glowing orange in that darkness. I had walked straight into the trap. Thank you, anger!

"Come in."

I hesitated. I could be at my car inside what, five or six seconds. More than enough time to—

I heard the car keys jangle as they hit the floor somewhere in the blackness of my lounge. I sighed and swore under my breath.

The first question sprang into my mind: What do you want? But that was verging on cliché, and even under this kind of pressure, there was no way I would ask it.

"Step inside and close the door."

It was a female voice. Quiet, just above a whisper. It was so quiet I could easily hear the mechanism inside the gun as she cocked it. I went cold from the inside out, like someone had just flushed out my system with tap water. I no longer felt quite right; I felt a tremor running throughout my body, and it wasn't one that just came and went; this bastard stayed there.

You know how you sometimes shake after a confrontation with someone who queue-jumped at McDonald's? A bit of mouthing off can do that to you; it's the adrenaline, the body preparing itself for a fight over a cheeseburger and large fries. Well, that kind of tremble was going on right now.

I stepped inside. Maybe if I'd just run I could have made it. Who knows?

"Close it."

Your going to die tonight.

I stared at the orange glow, feeling quite hollow in the chest.

"Now."

It slammed shut and she turned on the lamp I keep over by my armchair. So she hadn't cut the juice to the entire house, just taken out the lounge bulb maybe or flicked the fuse for the lighting circuit.

'What do you want?' tried to get out again. "Can I have one of those?" I nodded to the cigarette, trying to keep things cool. "And a coffee? Would you like one?" The lamp was behind her and so I couldn't see her very well, just a glowing silhouette with smoke drifting through it. She was sitting on the arm of my chair, cigarette seemingly dangling from her mouth, left hand holding a pistol pointing right at me. The light glinted off it, and overall it looked like something from a gangster movie, somewhere in New York maybe, around prohibition.

Except this was real. It was here, and it was now. I swallowed, the shaking worsened.

"Go on," she said, "talk your way out of this—"

"Do you mind if I smoke? I mean, if you're going to kill me, the least you can do is let me—"

She stood up quickly, as though she had a spring under her arse, and the speed she came at me almost knocked me off-balance. She was in my face. I could feel the muzzle up against the back of my neck, and she pulled me forward by my t-shirt so she could reach my face. Her lips moved against my cheek, and her hot breath leaked into my mouth as I tried to breathe. All the time she twitched the muzzle, boring it into my neck.

Not quite so cool now. I didn't realise it, but my eyes were shut tight. Any hope I had of smoothing my way to an graceful escape vanished.

"Funny man, eh?" she snarled.

My eyes snapped open.

"Gonna wise-talk me? Treat me like shit, Collins?" She screamed in my ear and then hit me on the back of the neck with the butt of the gun. I was on the floor, already in pain, when she kicked me in the kidney.

Any thoughts of being wise or of being brave or of being some kind of James Bond hero who could talk cool, ran away pretty fucking quickly. I was scared. I was submissive. And then it happened: that fucking question that made me as weak and as predictable as every other bastard on this planet just fell out of my mouth. "What do you want!" I hated myself.

From behind a shielding hand I looked up at her as she stood over me, panting. The light was still poor, but I could see she had blood on her. All down one arm, across her face and neck. What the fuck was going on?

One thing that struck me about all this was how it must be personal. I know how stupid that sounds, but think about it; if this had been a contract killing she would have killed me by now, no preamble, no messing about, no opportunity for James Bond to wrangle his way free, just pull the trigger and hit pay day.

But she hadn't done that; she was waiting for something, she wanted something from me, even if it was only to hear me beg – and hell would freeze over first, pal – or even if was just an explanation of something I'd done or said... she *wanted* something from me.

I had power.

I watched her, and there was something familiar... "Who are you?"

She didn't answer me, just kicked me again in the back. This time she got me right on the spine and it sent me into a spasm of pain that made me writhe on the floor. I didn't scream, I was too busy trying to catch my breath – it was like diving into the ocean, how it leaves you breathless for all the wrong reasons. It hurt like a bitch.

She retreated somewhere nearer the lamp and I caught a glimpse of her profile. Eventually, the agony lessened and a silence permeated the room like blood dispersing in water. I delved inside my jacket pocket for my cigarettes. Despite the pain, I still craved a smoke and I lit the bastard and puffed away, staring at her defiantly. I sat up, leaning back on one hand, leg casually bent like I was an advert for Burton's, trying not to let my fear show itself.

And she stared at me. Not blinking.

That's when the penny finally dropped and I gasped. Her eyes, large, dark and deep, gave nothing away; it's as if they were a barrier to what lay beneath rather than a window into her soul. 'Funny man' came at me from somewhere distant, a memory that I'd almost succeeded in erasing. You'd have thought it would have come to me straight away.

Alex was her name, and she was a fucking psycho.

As she moved around the table to stub out her cigarette, the lamp shone directly on her for the first time, and I saw that she'd changed considerably since I'd known her. She'd turned Goth; her smooth brown hair was now a matted black mess; she'd smothered black eye-liner on her upper and lower lids, making her large black eyes seem massive, and the black lipstick smeared all down her face turned her into an apprentice voodoo priestess.

Out of all the clues though – the voice, the familiar hand writing, the propensity for violence – it was the dead guy, John Tyler, who'd reminded me of her the most. The bite marks I'd photographed on some domestic violence victim who wore red Nike trainers. She did that to me once. I smoked quickly.

She half-smiled because she could see that I'd finally remembered her. It must have been a buzz for her.

"Nothing's changed, Alex," I said. "You still can't fucking spell." That would either kill me or cure the situation.

It didn't have the desired effect, and I reflected that it might have been the wrong approach. She walked over, leaned in close and spat in my face. That was enough; frightened or not, that was about all I could take from the mad cow. I dropped the cigarette, and stood, despite her pushing me, and despite her throwing a decent punch into the side of my head. I rocked a little but was able to get a grip on her jacket, and as I began to lose balance, dragged her with me. We teetered and then hit the deck in a tangle of limbs that would have been comedic under any other circumstances. This was no sitcom though.

She was breathing hard, almost rasping, her body countering the drugs I guessed she'd had. Everything went still and I held my breath, mouth open, eyes wide. The gun felt cold under my chin, and I won't lie, I was shitting myself. My grip on her slackened and, lying on my back, I raised my hands slowly into the air and watched the crazy look in her dead eyes. My heart stuttered.

I noticed that the smeared lipstick wasn't smeared lipstick at all. It was a thick coating of blood that was beginning to flake off like she was shedding a layer of reptilian skin.

I swallowed. I had no idea what she was planning to do next, but I seriously doubted I was going to get that coffee.

She pushed the muzzle harder into my throat. My heart rattled, and a pulse of dread skewered me.

"Close your eyes."

I tried to swallow again, but the gun was so hard into my throat that I could barely breathe let alone swallow. I croaked out the words, "What turned you into a fucking lunatic?" The blood around her mouth cracked as she screamed with all the ferocity of a woman being torn apart, physically and mentally. It was the most horrendous sound I've ever heard and it went on and on and her breath was hot and sour. Just before she bit into my face, she pushed the muzzle even harder and I braced myself, scrabbling backwards against it, clawing at the carpet.

She fired the gun.

— The Bite —

After the flash, the world turned utterly black and the ringing in my ears made me scream. She was laughing and when she lifted her head I could see more blood – *my* blood – dripping from her chin.

My face was on fire and my eyes were watering so badly I could barely open them. I could feel blood trickling down my neck. She really was a psycho bitch! The bullet had gone straight through the front door.

As she laughed I blinked away the tears and the blackness in my vision parted. I could see her front teeth, how the upper canines lay at an angle almost behind the incisors, and the lower canines were twisted to hell like someone fucked up a card shuffle.

She looked down at me, still laughing, holding the gun at me with one hand and gripping my t-shirt with the other as I stared back unbelieving, still in shock. And then she started to grind. Her pelvis gyrated on my dick like we were a couple of teenagers getting randy. Trust me, I wasn't in the mood for randy!

"Do you think there's a chance for us, Eddie? Huh, to be happy like we was?"

I was shaking. "I think we need to talk," I whispered, wincing as the sting in my cheek grew hotter. My own voice sounded muffled like someone had tuned out all the treble and there was just the bass left.

Someone else had unplugged Mad Bitch and plugged in Romantic Vampire Slut. She leaned in close looking at me, studying me, black eyes flitting between my own. She leaned in and kissed me.

What the hell do you do when an armed psycho kisses you? No really, what do you do? If you kiss back, she's got you; if you resist, she's angry. Either way, she's got you.

I'd read somewhere that some people get off on torture, that they get horny just before the big event – and the big event I was worried about involved her trigger finger, and my brains dripping down the wallpaper. Not an ideal end to the day.

Your going to die tonight.

She slid her tongue in my mouth and I tasted my own blood.

I nearly freaked out; it was all I could do stop from vomiting. At least I knew where I stood with the Mad Bitch; this was scary on a whole new level.

"I could move in. If you like."

She tried to kiss me again, and I spat out the vile taste of blood and got a stabbing reminder of the damage she'd done to my face.

"Hey," she soothed, kindness shimmering in her eyes as she stroked my good cheek with her thumb. I could hear the stubble under her nail. "What's the matter?"

My first reaction was to laugh, but I choked it immediately. I focused my mind on the death threat and realised this evening wouldn't end well for at least one of us.

Be tactful, was the only advice I could give myself. "I could write you a list."

She sat up and the kindness left her eyes. "What?"

"I mean it's pretty difficult to think with you waving a gun around."

She relaxed, took the gun from my throat and just sat there on my groin with a delightful smile on her wretched face. She was a rose made of arsenic.

I last saw Alex when I was eighteen years old. At eighteen you know everything there is to know about the world. It's only when someone comes along who isn't on your own wavelength that you begin to learn new things. Pain was one of the things Alex taught me. Mental pain to begin with quickly followed by physical pain.

Her dad had thrown her out.

She'd got pregnant, see, and then miscarried, and he finally disowned her when she began stealing from him. He was ashamed of her, didn't talk about her with his friends, stopped talking about her to her mother, and didn't even declare her on some fancy job application he filled out.

He didn't want the embarrassment, she had told me. I never met him, but he sounded like a prick. It was hard for her, but she hadn't done anything to escape the spiral of decay and self-hatred she found herself in. If anything, she'd propagated it, almost relished being inside this maelstrom, and from it developed a wonderful reputation as a wretched whore who'd cut your throat and guzzle your life-blood if you so much as farted within earshot.

"What?" She was staring at me again; kind of amused to find me in thought, I suppose.

"Nothing," I said, listening as my hearing came back towards normal.

"Go on, whatcha thinking?"

"Get off me, Alex, you're starting to piss me off."

She gripped my t-shirt, and gave me that look again.

I sighed, "I was thinking about us." The smile returned, and I couldn't keep up with her changing emotions any longer; each comment was a game of chance, a spin of a revolver's cylinder.

"Been doing that a lot too. Thinking about us, I mean." She let go of the t-shirt. "I was there, you know. When you were photographing him, and it got me thinking."

"Who?"

"Who what?"

"When I was photographing who?"

"Him. My ex, John."

"John Tyler?" I tried to sit up a bit, but it was difficult with a lunatic crushing your nuts. "When? Tonight?"

"I meant when you were at our house photographing his injuries. His bite marks!" She laughed like a banshee on speed, and a fresh shudder skittered through me. She was so fucking unpredictable it was scary. "I watched you from the other room. I was remembering you, and how you used to fuck. You were an animal, Eddie. Could've ripped off your clothes there and then." She grinned and winked, but coming from her, it was no compliment. It just added fuel to my misery.

I *wondered* why he'd been so timid. I remember thinking how I pitied him but how he really ought to grow a spine. No wonder he was timid, if *she* was there watching over him; bet he was bricking himself. If I'd known she was there, I'd have been bricking myself too. Like I was now.

"And yes, I was there tonight too. Watched you arguing with the man in the suit."

I took a long slow blink: I *knew* I was being watched, I knew it! I tried to remain calm – actually what I mean is that I tried to reclaim some calmness. "Why do you bite people?" My top lip curled at the revulsion of it and I could feel my stinging cheek begin to swell.

She shrugged. "It's hard to dance with a demon on your back."

"Kind of fucking reply is that?"

"What, you my therapist, now?"

I said nothing, just stared, demanding an answer.

She sighed, and then her eyes sparkled, "It gives me a thrill. It makes me feel in charge." She sat back on me as though she'd satisfied my curiosity.

"It makes you feel superior?"

She glanced upwards as though contemplating.

"You like to be in control of people." I studied her as she stared into me. "You like to be on top."

She smiled.

"It's not funny."

"It is funny when you try to psycho-analyse me. But I'm no subject in a fucking book, Eddie. I'm just me, and I—"

"You love to dominate people. You dominated John Tyler, you ruled and crushed him till he was just a shell with no opinion and no self-esteem."

The smile vanished. "Bollocks."

I recalled how *I'd* grown a spine back when I was eighteen. I finished with her because she bit me on the neck, right where the jugular is. At first it had been very arousing and back then it didn't take a fella like me long to get turned on. It was such a turn on that I had her jeans undone and was working them down her legs in no time at all, when she bit deeper.

She bit hard enough to stop me in my tracks, fingers paused, not daring to touch her again. I held my breath and my fervour perished pretty fucking quickly. Not a turn on any longer.

"I love to see someone in pain that's just the other side of ecstasy. Just before it gets unbearable." She paused and took a quivering breath, "But mostly I like to see them on the other side of unbearable."

I remembered how it *really* began to hurt. I can remember the huge pressure in my chest, how it boiled and how I could do nothing as her teeth cut. And how her jaws clamped so tightly that I wanted to scream but couldn't. Daren't move in case she bit even deeper.

"There isn't no feeling like it. And when I'm pissed off, it's my drug."

And in the same way she'd bitten into my face minutes ago, it had a debilitating effect; it caused complete sublimation, like a paralysis so she could punch and kick. Which she did.

"Coke not in fashion anymore?"

Her face changed again and inwardly I groaned. Her eyes narrowed, the silly grin that almost made her endearing faded and just vanished. The gun I'd almost forgotten about reappeared and as I eyed it she punched me on the jaw right where she'd bitten through the bristly flesh. I became her rodeo ride for a few minutes as I bucked against the pain.

Just as I'd done all those years ago, I grew my spine again.

I had reached the point where I would rather she just get on and shoot me dead than carry on with this fucking torture any longer. With that feeling came a new viewpoint, one that was prepared to take more risks. I think she saw the change in me because she recoiled, but it was already too late, I was furious.

I whipped my hips upwards and she tipped forward, releasing the pressure on my arms that were pinned beneath her knees. She flipped over my head without having time to curse let alone hit me with the damned gun again. And in a frantic scrabble that lasted no more than a few seconds, I'd positioned myself more or less on my knees at her side, and punched her as hard as I could in the side of the head.

She hit the floor like a sack of shit and I rocked back on my heels seething at the pain in my knuckles. I rolled onto my backside breathing hard like I'd just run to the car from the house. She lay there with her black hair just a messy tussle over her head, her limbs limp and the gun glinting by the lamp light a yard or two away.

That's how I'd grown a spine, and that's how I'd left her all those years ago. I'd hit back – physically and metaphorically. Just like her dad had taught her that's what life was about: a hitting competition to see who gives in first.

The Note

— The Truth —

"You bastard!"

I sat on the toilet and smiled down at her as I gingerly dabbed a ball of dampened toilet paper against my cheek. It was throbbing, and I had a headache. "You started it."

She pulled at the kettle cable that I'd used to tie her to the copper pipes running along the bathroom wall. She looked uncomfortable, lying half on her side, hands up in the air.

"It's because of you that I can't have a coffee."

"Go fuck yourself."

I looked at my watch. It was three-thirty but I didn't feel the least bit tired; I guess adrenaline keeps you wide awake and ready to fight again. "How come you got together with John Tyler?" I knew why she'd chosen to hook up with him: he was weak, timid, and she found controlling him very easy. And enjoyable.

She ignored the question, stopped struggling and stared hatred up at me. "Can you slacken this off? My hands are turning blue."

"Would you like your gun back as well?"

She pulled at the cable some more, tried to kick out at me, and it was all I could do stop laughing at her – she looked like a petulant child, bottom lip out, the full works, including tears. She yanked at the cable and I saw the pipes bend ever so slightly as the veins in her neck stood out and she gritted her teeth.

"You're wasting your time," I said. "I had the plumbing certified to British Standard Mad Cow Restraint Class 1."

"You won't be fucking laughing when I get free."

Another shudder skittered through me. But I shrugged, trying to appear nonchalant when in reality I was still very much on edge. Okay, I'd taken the gun away from her, but she was charged full of nervous energy and a fury that was pure and completely uninhibited. I made sure to keep away from the kicking feet, but I couldn't escape her eyes, and how they penetrated mine to such a depth that I had to push the toilet paper harder into my cheek to break the spell.

It didn't take too long before she exhausted herself though. She settled down, panting, recovering her strength, but her eyes remained on mine throughout.

"Why did you write me the note?"

When she smiled up at me I went cold again.

"I'm on a mission," she whispered. "I need to be free of you lot; all the men that have fucked me over all my life."

"What?"

"I'm a mess, Eddie. I am a mess because of you. And them others like you. It's not my fault."

"I've never met anyone as strong as you. You could achieve anything you wanted to achieve. You can manipulate people better than a politician can! So how can you say it's not your fault? How can you take no responsibility for what you've become? Why is it always someone else's fault? That's the ultimate fucking cop-out." I didn't want to be so harsh, but it was true; it's easier to blame someone else than deal with your own failures. "If you'd channelled that strength—"

"What do you know? You don't know me; you don't know what I've been—"

"I mean, that tells me you know you're... you're aware you have mental problems—"

She screamed, "I know that! Don't you fucking think I know that! That's what they told me, that I got problems, that I got to take this drug and that drug..." She stared at me still, eyes on fire. "But it's not a cure."

"So what is?"

Now it was her turn to look away as though she dare not share the secret. But she didn't need to speak the words – she'd already written them down, once on paper, and now again right across her face.

"Killing me won't set you free, Alex. Just like killing John Tyler when he tried to fight back by involving the police didn't set you free."

She froze.

"I'm not stupid."

It seemed to hit her like it was a revelation, like it had never even occurred to her. The tears that came now were genuine, her whole body racked against them but they won and she gave in and collapsed against her arms, pulling her legs up, curling into a ball.

"I just don't understand it." I dabbed a bit more, speaking now more to myself than her. "Why not just kill me? Why go through all that shit? Fist fighting, biting a fucking hole in my cheek!" I sighed, "You had the gun on me. Pop," I said, pointing a pistol finger. "Easy as that."

She didn't answer me, just cried. Why face your failures when you can cry over them instead?

It was too late for sympathy though; nothing I could do to help her. She'd never be free, and even if she killed me and all the other men who'd shunned her, she'd forever walk among them, chained to them, and no amount of crying would redeem her. I think she knew that too.

I looked at my watch again. Three-forty. What was taking them so bloody long?

"But if you were intent on killing me," I continued, as though casually chatting over a pint in the local, "why send me a note telling me?"

Between sobs, her eyes turned to slits and she snarled, "To make you suffer." A long string of spittle glided to the tiled floor. "You haven't got no idea what it's like to get rejected by everyone you hook up with."

"Biting them probably didn't help."

"Shut up."

"Just a thought."

"Shut up!"

So far as I could tell there were three main men she felt angry towards. Her dad, who'd kicked her out and left her to fend for herself because she was an embarrassment to him; John Tyler who dared to call the police and enter the domestic violence playground, and me. I was the first boyfriend she'd had who had thrown her away. I didn't feel regret over it; everyone 'hooks' up with people and then parts from them as they find out they don't quite fit together anymore.

It's just one of those life-learning things, and you have to get used to that. If you don't... well if you don't, you end up tied to some bloke's plumbing crying into the crook of your arm because the world has been too cruel for you to bear.

I don't mean to make it all sound so flippant, but really. I sighed, and mouthed, "Get a grip, Alex."

Trouble was, she heard me, and her sorrowful crying stopped dead. She became still, glaring at me as though I was the enemy, the destroyer of her magnificent dream. Her days of domination were gone. I hated myself a little bit then as she spat up at me again.

Alex put her shoulder against the wall and pulled against the electrical cable. The pipes flexed further and the cable dug into her wrists so much I thought it'd cut right through to the bone. It made me wince, and I knew she was furious with me for not understanding. She screamed in a rage that sent a prickle up my throbbing spine.

I often wonder what would have happened next if I'd kept my mouth shut, or if I'd sympathised with her a bit more. I wonder if there had been a chance I could have pulled her around from this emotional turmoil she rode through. Was there ever a chance I could have convinced her that life wasn't out to get her? It's just there to be lived, and then it ends.

But I hadn't been sympathetic enough; she pulled and she pulled and then, as I stood up, there was an urgent knocking at the door. Alex didn't hear it, she was too busy growling and screaming again to notice. I slid out of the room and closed the door quietly behind me.

— The End —

It was almost four o'clock, and nowhere near dawn, but in the dimming light of the Discovery headlights, I could see the dayglow stripes of a police car through the patterned glass in the front door, and I sighed my relief. When I opened the door though, my sigh dried up and a groan stamped it dead.

"Where is she?"

"Dibble. What the fuck are you doing here?" He and Bashed-Crab stood only a foot or two away, keeping dry under the porch, and behind them were two armed officers whom I knew from the nick. I half nodded at them; they folded their arms and leaned against their ARV oblivious to the incessant rain. Behind it was Dibble's plain car.

"What happened to your face?" he asked.

"Rough sex with an Alsatian." I pulled the door against me so he couldn't squeeze past. Don't get me wrong, I didn't owe Alex anything, except a bill for a new door, but I didn't want to hand her over to this twat.

He would see she got a rough ride just because that's what made him the big man he was inside his own mind. He liked to score off others' misery and for a man with no soul, being a cop was the perfect job – lots of misery within easy reach.

"Is she here or not? If you're wasting my time, I'll—"

"Shut up, you fuckwit. I'm off the clock so show me some respect or get this slammed in your face."

The two armed officers smiled at each other.

I looked over Dibble's shoulder at them and said, "You wanna come in and prove the weapon?"

They stepped forward, gently slid past Dibble, and I opened the door for them.

"Over there," I said, "on the little table." They disappeared from my view. I faced Dibble as more shite fell out of his mouth.

"You reported a murder suspect in your house."

"I did. Let the two armed officers take her into custody, and you can stay with me and write some lies in your pocket notebook."

"She's mine," he said between clenched teeth.

Well of course she was his; he wanted the collar, he wanted to make Inspector before the year was out and this was a good rung on the promotional ladder. "You shouldn't be here," I said. "You'll compromise the case – you've been to the murder scene. It's called contamination."

"*You've* been to the scene!" He looked at Bashed-Crab for support. Oh how victorious he sounded.

"I didn't have a choice her turning up at my house, did I? Think about it for a second and when the penny drops, you can piss off back to the nick and ridicule a shoplifter."

"I am duty Sergeant for this Division, so please step aside, Mr Collins, and let me do my job before I pull you for obstruction."

As I thought about it, I could hear Alex kicking and screaming in the bathroom behind me. She hadn't calmed down by the sounds of it, and I wondered if she knew they were here for her. I stepped aside and let him in.

He smiled at me and I wanted to pull his face off and stuff it up his arse.

He licked his lips and I could see how eager he was to get her in cuffs and bundle her into the back of his car. I could imagine him singing *We are the Champions* on his way to the nick.

"What makes you think she's the dropout's killer?"

"He has bite marks on him. She bites," I said, pointing to my cheek. "She's also his partner in a domestic violence case. His name's John Tyler. I photographed his injuries a few days ago and she admitted to hiding there while I did it."

"That it?"

"She's also covered in blood that I think will come back as his."

His eyes widened and he looked again at the bathroom door. The noise coming from in there was horrendous, but it didn't put Dibble off, he looked more enthusiastic than ever, and you could see him struggling to control that sickly smile again. Perhaps he was hoping for a bit of a struggle, maybe he could acquire a bruise or two, maybe a fat lip that could turn him into an instant hero and grant him a commendation.

He made me sick.

"She's tied to the pipes with an electrical cable, so there's no need to be rough with her." I stood before him, blocking his way to the bathroom door. "Why don't I go in first and see if I can calm her down a bit?"

"You tied her up?"

"You've seen my cheek!"

"So move out of the fucking way and let me do my job?"

"She's distressed, cut her a break."

"Move."

"Don't take your anger at me out on her."

"Last time, Collins. Move."

There really was nothing more I could say or do. Alex was in his hands now, at his mercy. I pitied her.

He paused at the door for a moment, listening to the riot in there, and then his hand was on the doorknob. That's when I noticed the water trickling out from under the bathroom door, spreading into the carpet by our feet, and I could hear it spraying like a fountain inside, like someone had turned on the shower.

It dawned on me what had happened and I tried to reach for him as he burst into the bathroom. I was right behind him. I had wanted to say 'stop', but that word was kind of redundant now.

I saw the broken pipes spewing a fan of water against the wall beneath the sink, and right out across the floor. Over the sink was a window, now wide open. The venetian blind was a tattered mess across the sink, draping over its edge like metal fingers. My toothbrush and toothpaste, my aftershave and razor crushed and scattered.

The first fronds of daylight leached through the naked glass. A little part of me – the part that hadn't received the death threat – cheered her escape. I hoped she got away from here. And most importantly for me and my burning cheek, I hoped she stayed the hell away.

Dibble spun on his heels, and glared at me; I'm sure out of the corner of his eye he saw his commendation floating out of the bathroom like a paper boat. "You fucking idiot, Collins." He looked past me and yelled to his sidekick, "Get after her, Chris! Make sure you get her!" Bashed-Crab and one of the armed cops ran out of the front door; one went left the other right. To me he said, "I'm gonna have you for obstruction."

"What the hell did *I* do?"

He turned and went back into the bathroom. "Stood in my way while she escaped—"

She appeared from behind the open door and plunged a knife into Dibble's chest right up to the handle.

Her ragged hair was wet through. Her hands were still bound together, and now I knew why she'd tried to get her legs up to the pipes where her hands were tied so she could slide the knife out of her boot.

The Note

She pulled the knife out and screamed into his face until all the strength left his legs and he just folded, collapsing to his knees on the wet floor like a man made of paper.

There he stayed for a second or two as though unsure of which way to fall. I was mesmerised – not in a good way. My mouth was open, and I stared at Alex as she screamed her fury into the world, her face taut, yet anguished eyes closed behind a thousand folds of agony. Dibble's blood soaked her chest, and her own blood dripped from her wrist wound to disperse in the shallow torrent at her feet.

Dibble finally made up his mind and toppled backwards, splashing to the lounge floor, almost colliding with me. And then he was still, staring up at the ceiling, never quite having made Inspector.

She screamed and water gushed.

And then there was just gushing water. She stood there in silence, her face a twist of consternation, a mess of black make-up smeared into contortions. Her eyes were afraid; they were terrified because she was almost free.

Almost.

Water dripped from her clothes and from her face. Red water danced over white tiles, and more joined it, swirling from the dead man. She stared at him, "Dad," she whispered, "*this* is what it feels like to be disowned." And then she looked back at me.

"Get down!"

I heard the officer behind me and didn't turn to ask questions. I just folded my legs and hit the deck as he discharged his Taser.

A pair of sparking wires, hair-thin, appeared over my head and Alex screamed afresh as the barbs pierced her skin. In a spasm of convulsions she too hit the floor. The knife skittered away. I lay motionless on the wet carpet, rigid with fear and disorientated, panting, not daring to move. I know how un-heroic that sounds, but I was on the edge, and had been there all fucking night, so cut me some slack. I'm allowed to be scared!

I turned my head, feeling the cold water against my ear, and I looked at Dibble. I saw the bloom of blood on his shirt, how it had run across his chest and down to be carried away in the water, swirling. But mostly I saw the utter disbelief on his face: *How could this happen to me? I'm invincible. I've been alive all my life. And soon I'll know what it's like... not to be. This wasn't in the script.*

The copper was at my side, "Okay, Eddie?"

I croaked, "Fucking wonderful." I snapped away from Dibble's shocked face and slowly got to my wet feet. I saw the copper grab the knife, and throw it from the bathroom out here into the lounge. He checked she was okay, made sure she was breathing, and pulled her away from the wall. "She played me," I said.

"You were next."

I pictured her panting, relieved one of us was dead, but still craving the final retribution. Only I could give her that, and it's what she'd wanted all along. I had stood there, immobile, hypnotised – *traumatised* – by her black eyes and the black, streaked makeup on her cheeks, a look on my face similar to the one Dibble's now wore; of disbelief and incomprehension as she sank the blade into my throat and twisted—

"Did she say what I thought she said?"

I blinked, and dabbed fingertips at my neck. "She planned it all." I became aware that my cheek was on fire again.

"Crazy bitch."

Crazy maybe, but clever, and devious. This was why she didn't just kill me outright. She knew I'd bring her father to her. "This carpet is ruined," I said, dazed, trying to fish a cigarette from my jacket pocket. When I did it was wet through, and just disintegrated in my trembling fingers. I threw the packet away and looked up hopefully at him, nerves wrecked.

He shook his head, "I don't smoke."

"Fuck, what's up with you?" I shouted.

The other armed officer and Bashed-Crab ran back inside, and when they saw the scene, they gawped at one another, radios blaring all kinds of crap about an escaped prisoner, and about getting the helicopter up and getting the dogs out, and then... then it all got too much and I screamed at them to shut the fuck up!

* * *

I found myself in the kitchen ready to make a strong coffee only to discover that the kettle had no cable.

I closed my eyes at the injustice of it all.

"Two out of three ain't bad, Alex." I felt again at my neck, unable to shake the image of her sticking that blade in me, and my fingers came away clean. Trembling, but clean. And, you'll probably laugh, but I felt emotional; I felt like crying because I'd wriggled out of death one more time. It wasn't like this in the movies where the hero picks himself up, refuses medical treatment, and goes on to chase down the last of the baddies to some upbeat musical score.

Well it wasn't like that for me. I couldn't believe how fucking lucky I'd been as I shuffled back into the lounge.

He was still there, dead on my floor like a fat draft-excluder, legs bent beneath him in the last and best limbo dance he'd ever do.

Like a handkerchief, it protruded from his breast pocket.

I stared at it.

Around the room, commotion ruled. Bashed-Crab was asking if he should perform CPR, his voice unnaturally squeaky, and I could tell that one of the armed officers was considering whether to slap him from his reverie. The other armed officer scratched his groin as he spoke into his radio. Voices everywhere, radio comms everywhere, a siren growing louder. But it was silence to me.

I licked my dry lips, and told my stupid legs to get me over to Dibble without buckling beneath me. I don't know how, but they did. And I stared at him as those around me blurred into various degrees of shade, like ghosts drinking ectoplasm.

The handkerchief wasn't a handkerchief, of course. I bent, took it from his pocket. I carefully unfolded the note. It was almost identical to the one she'd sent to me, complete with stab marks.

Your going to die tonight.

If only she'd used a dictionary!

It didn't work. I tried to rid myself of the nerves – call it what you will – with a little humour. It had always worked in the past; it was my thing, it was my soothing counsellor's voice, it was the pat on the back, it was the kick up the arse. It was everything I needed to shake the shit off and get back to normal.

Except this time it didn't work.

Why?

You ever had that feeling of being watched, and when you turn around, no one's there? Spooky, isn't it? It happened to me just then. This time, I did turn and looked right into her eyes. They were wide, red-rimmed, inside a void of smudged black makeup. She came at me like a demon, a scream from her twisted mouth that nailed me to the spot like I was imminent road-kill. Her talons were almost at my throat, ready to tear it out.

I could imagine Bashed-Crab and the two coppers, their lives on pause, slowly turning to see her rushing at me, powerless to prevent my death.

I was mesmerised by her. And I think it was a reflex action that caused me to bring up my arms, probably in a defensive attempt. But your mind and body are marvellous when you leave them alone to just get on with things that happen too fast for you to even begin contemplating a course of action.

Without my conscious command, I swung a fist at those beautifully horrific eyes and made contact. I threw the blow so hard that I spun myself right off balance and landed at Bashed-Crab's feet.

Alex spiralled through the air like a dead ballerina and landed in a moaning heap by my damaged front door. Within moments, she felt the restraining knee of an armed officer as he fed her wrists into his cuffs.

I was numb as she looked at me. Her eyes, they didn't blink. She smiled at me. "I'll never forget you, Eddie," she whispered. "Don't forget me, eh? Because one day, I'll be around the very next corner." She was hauled to her feet, her eyes never leaving mine.

"Just a minute," I said to the copper. I stood and crossed the floor, carpet squelching under my feet. I was within a foot or so of her, staring into the chasms of her eyes, and smiled, "Don't suppose you've got a spare cigarette?"

Author's Note

I write crime thrillers, and have done since 1996, about the same time I became a CSI here in Yorkshire. All of my books are set in or around our biggest city of Leeds. Sometimes I go wandering into the stunning countryside though and drag its beauty screaming into the pages of one of my books where it collides with the ugliness of death.

I don't write formulaic crime fiction; each story is hand-crafted and nurtured to give you a unique flavour of what CSIs encounter in real life. Every book is rich with forensic insight but that insight never drowns the story; it's there to enhance your enjoyment only.

My thrillers live inside the police domain; they have detectives and uniformed officers, but they're predominantly about CSIs (or SOCOs as we used to be known). Come and live with them as they go about their sometimes unenviable tasks, and listen to the language they speak, see the things they see, and experience the emotions they feel.

So pull on your nitrile gloves and your face mask, get comfy, and read on.

Get in touch.

For further information, or to sign up for my Reader's Club, please visit Andrew-Barrett.co.uk. And if you'd like to comment to me directly, I'd be delighted to hear from you on Facebook (and so would Eddie Collins) and Twitter.

You can make a big difference.

Did you enjoy this book? I hope you did. Reviews are the most powerful tools in my arsenal when it comes to getting attention for my work. I don't have the financial muscle of a New York publisher; I can't take out full page ads in the newspaper, or put posters on the subway.

But I have something more effective than that, and it's something those publishers would kill to get their hands on.

A committed and loyal bunch of readers.

Honest reviews of my books help bring them to the attention of other readers. If you've enjoyed this book I would be very grateful if you could spend just five minutes leaving a review (it can be as short as you like).

Reader's Club Download Offer

GET TWO FREE BEST-SELLERS AND A FREE
SHORT STORY.

Building a relationship with readers is the very best thing about writing. I occasionally send details of new releases, special offers, and other news relating to the Roger Conniston, and Eddie Collins series.

Sign up to the Reader's Club and get these **free** goodies:

A Long Time Dead, the first in the Roger Conniston trilogy.
The Third Rule, the first book in the Eddie Collins series – a 600-page best-seller.
The Lift, a first person short story where you can climb inside Eddie's head and see life as he does.

Books by Andrew Barrett

A Long Time Dead – SOCO Roger Conniston Book One

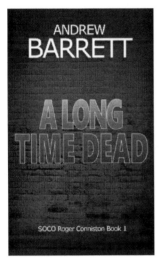

How much trust can you put in forensic evidence?
They discovered her naked body with a puncture wound to her neck and blood everywhere. And brutal though her death was, this was the second such case West Yorkshire Police had running. Both unsolved. Until they found that one elusive piece of evidence.

"I've never read a more authentic and detailed crime thriller."

Get *A Long Time Dead* here

Stealing Elgar – SOCO Roger Conniston
Book Two

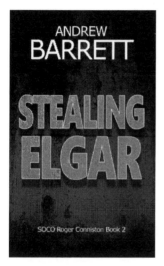

"Examining crime scenes was never supposed to get personal."

Roger Conniston has a lot to prove and a lot to protect. He's up against an ex-bare-knuckle fighter called Hades who is planning the most audacious robbery in England's history.

For Hades, the success of this 'one last job' is paramount. He's planned it in meticulous detail, from the explosive diversions that will shock the nation, to the selection of his team and the weapons they'll use.

Roger is faced with a decision: continue working with the police or cut the ties and venture out alone to stop Hades and secure everything he cares about.

"This is an intensely gripping book, though very dark in tone."

Get *Stealing Elgar* here

No More Tears – SOCO Roger Conniston
Book Three

"It'll screw you up into a tiny ball of hatred and then spit you out into a cell."

SOCO Roger Conniston, always believed in the law. Not now though. Now he believes only in himself. He has business with people who have no right being alive, and if success costs him everything they left him with, he'll happily pay. For him, this is a journey into places he didn't know existed, encountering people so violent and determined that he almost weakens. The question facing Roger is: how far dare you go?

Old enemies – and new ones – backstab and double-cross each other to get to Roger.

Deceit, friendship, greed, and honour, are all played out in this concluding episode.

"A superb piece of writing to end the trilogy."

Get *No More Tears* here

The Third Rule – CSI Eddie Collins
Book One

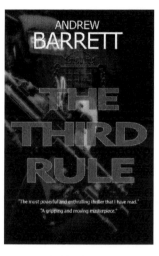

When they accuse you of murder, you'd better hide, run, or fight.

The Third Rule is England's new infallible capital punishment where absolute proof of guilt is not required. There's always a queue at the Slaughter House doors.

CSI Eddie Collins hasn't killed anyone, but he knows who has. That's why he's on the Slaughter House list, and when a government hunter tracks him down, Eddie has to fight or die.

"If you want to kill serious crime, you have to kill serious criminals." Sir George Deacon, Minster of Justice.

"Gripping from start to finish. Real life characters who are believable and interesting, great plot and a read that easily compares with Jeffrey Deaver, Lee Child, James Patterson, Patricia Cornwall and all the big names. Andrew is going places!"

Get *The Third Rule* here

Black by Rose – CSI Eddie Collins
Book Two

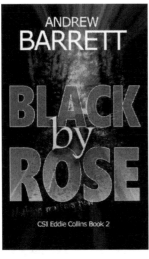

Black by Rose is the key to it all.

In a rage, CSI Eddie Collins leaves a murder scene, triggering a series of life changing events; but not only for him.

Operation Domino is the Major Crime Unit's investigation into gang boss, Slade Crosby, and the killing of an undercover officer. But when Eddie finds a gangland victim dead in his house, he confronts Crosby and instantly wishes he hadn't. There is a gun at his head. And no way out. Even the MCU cannot save him.

Tampered evidence halts Domino's progress, and with Eddie out of the way, Crosby is in the clear.

How can Eddie escape death and nail Crosby before the killing starts again?

"This book kept on giving and kept me page turning."

Get *Black by Rose* here

Sword of Damocles – CSI Eddie Collins Book Three

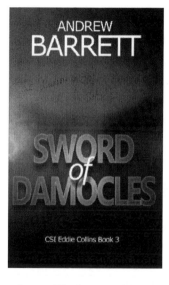

Some secrets never die.

When the remains of a woman are found in a burnt-out car, CSI Eddie Collins teams up with his enemy, DI Benson, to untangle the knot of lies behind this apparent suicide.

As a CSI in the Major Crime Unit, Eddie is forced to lead a disintegrating team that he can't control or tolerate, as they go up against a killer who will do anything to protect his past, and profit from it.

Solving the problem is difficult enough, proving it is deadly.

"A fantastically plotted tale of secrets and lies played out through snappy writing by well-defined characters. Definitely another winner!"

Get _Sword of Damocles_ here

Ledston Luck – CSI Eddie Collins
Book Four

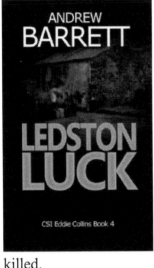

They say you can always trust a copper. They're lying.
They lied thirty years ago and they're still lying today.

A booby-trapped body in a long-abandoned chapel. A scene examination that goes horribly wrong. CSI Eddie Collins and DI Benson are injured and one of the team killed.

Eddie is heartbroken and guilt-ridden.

And angry.

"If you only read one novel this year make sure it's this one."

Get *Ledston Luck* here

The Lift – A CSI Eddie Collins Short Story

CSI Eddie Collins embarks on another ordinary day. But the people he meets in a lift prove that you should never make assumptions, never let preconceptions sway your judgement.

And never let down your guard.

"A masterclass in how to hook the reader and then rack up the tension level to 100 in no time at all."

Get *The Lift* here

Thanks...

Many thanks to my superb editors Kath Middleton and Graeme Bottomley, without whom *The Note* would not have turned out so well.

I would also to like to give a special mention to all of the wonderful bloggers who help authors and readers by sharing their views of our books.

And to some of the best groups on Facebook: The UK Crime Book Club run by David Gilchrist and Caroline Maston; the Eddie Collins Group, brimming with enthusiasm and support; and THE Book Club run by Tracy Fenton and her army, including the magnificent Helen Boyce – never too busy to listen to my pathetic pleas.

It would also be remiss of me not to mention and bow my head to the magnificent people in the Advance Reader's Team whose encouragement and help have no bounds – I'm **truly** grateful.

My warmest thanks to **you** for downloading this e-book, or for purchasing the paperback. Without your support none of this would be worth doing.

I reserve the biggest thanks of all for my lady, Sarah, without whom the sun would never rise.

The Note is dedicated to…

Bruce and Linda Jowitt

Original cover art used with kind permission of Susanne Ånes Ellingsen.